St
(Claire,)

Enjoy the
magic o
Pet adoption.

♡
S. Luida
Gunther

MW00981056

A Note About the SPCA

The Society For the Prevention of Cruelty To Animals (SPCA) is a non-profit organization that is dedicated to the welfare of animals. The great work they do is made possible because of individual contributions.

Please make a donation to your local SPCA or consider adopting a pet of your own. I adopted Toffee, a wonderful little dog, and best friend.

Thank you Santa Cruz SPCA.

Linda S. Gunther

This book is dedicated to my granddaughter, Kaitlyn who was a great help to me
in developing the characters and traits for both *Toffee and Esmerelda.*
Additionally, I'd like to thank the local SPCA staff and volunteers for giving their love to
all animals in their care. It is because of you, the volunteers who joyfully walk the path at
Seacliff Beach, that we now have this wonderful addition to our family.

May this heartfelt story encourage you to rescue a pet either through linking
with your local SPCA or Animal Rescue shelter.

Illustrations by Zsa-Zsa Venter
Edited by Laurel Ornitz

Esmerelda was nine years old.

She lived with her mom in a pastel blue house by the ocean.

Her dad was in the Army, stationed far away in another country.

Esmerelda's mom had inherited her grandpa's old house,

which sat just steps away from the beach in a seaside town called Seacliff.

"It's pretty, but do we have to live here?"

Esmerelda asked her mom, wishing she hadn't moved away from her friends.

Esmerelda could see the ocean waves and many sailboats
from her living room window. Looking out at the blue sea, she felt lonely.
It was summertime and she hadn't yet made any friends in their new
neighborhood.
School wasn't due to start until September and it was only
the beginning of July. Ugh, it's going to be a long summer,
Esmerelda thought.

Esmerelda liked to read stories about princesses and wizards,
so she spent a lot of time with her books.
She also liked to spread out on her lavender quilt
and sketch pictures of her dad and friends she missed
from her old neighborhood in Tempe, Arizona.

Sometimes she wrote letters or crafted cards to say that
she missed them. Still, she felt lonely.

Esmerelda liked music and played the saxophone almost every day.
Her mom seemed to brighten up whenever she heard the sound of the sax.
When playing, Esmerelda would think of her dad, who had taught her
lots of jazz tunes. When she blew into the sax,

Esmerelda could almost see her dad smiling and encouraging her to play.
"Go Ezzie, go, my sweet girl," he would say.
But when Esmerelda put down the sax,
she'd get sad and lonely again.

One day, while strolling on the beach with her mom, Esmerelda spotted three ladies walking three little dogs.

One of the dogs pulled toward Esmerelda. It was a spunky brown-and-white dog wearing a red jacket that had three words printed across the fabric: "PLEASE ADOPT ME."

Esmerelda's mom noticed the dog tugging, the long curly tail wagging furiously. "Is that dog really available for adoption?" her mom asked the ladies. Esmerelda's brown eyes opened wide in surprise.
"Yes, she sure is," one of the women replied, smiling.
Looking over at Esmerelda, she said, "Would you like to pet her?"
Esmerelda exclaimed, "Yes, please."

"I'm Sally," the woman continued, "and all three of these dogs are up for adoption at the local SPCA. If you hurry, maybe you can adopt this one. We didn't know her real name, so we named her Toffee, like the candy. We think she's about nine months old, but that's just an estimate of her age. She was a stray, picked up on the street in downtown Santa Cruz. No tags and nobody seems to be looking for her. She's been with us for over thirty days now, so she's adoptable."

The dog looked up as if recognizing her name and wagged her tail again, this time even faster. Sally picked up the dog and placed her in Esmerelda's arms.

"Oh Mom, I already love her," Esmerelda said, beaming.

"Can we adopt her? Can we?"

Her mom raised her eyebrows and said,

"Maybe. We can look into it."

SANTA CRUZ
SPCA
ADOPTION CENTER

They hurried home. Her mom sat down at her laptop, completed the
application, and printed it within minutes. Then they went off in the car,
zipping down the freeway headed for the SPCA office.

They arrived even before the ladies with the dogs got back from the beach.
"So, Toffee is the dog you want then?" a tall woman wearing
bright-green-rimmed eyeglasses asked. Esmerelda nodded.
"She sure is a cutie," the woman continued.
"We think she's a mix of Jack Russell Terrier and maybe some Beagle,
but we can't be absolutely sure with strays."

Esmerelda's face lit up when Toffee pranced through the doorway with the other dogs and the ladies.

The woman looked up from the application. "Ah, well, here they are now. Good timing!" she said. "Esmerelda, you and your mom will need to spend about thirty minutes with Toffee. That way, you'll find out if you really want her as your pet and we'll get to observe Toffee's behavior to see if she really wants you. Is that okay?"

Esmerelda suddenly felt nervous, but nodded eagerly.

"I'm betting it will be a good match between you and little Toffee. Take her outside in the dog yard if you like," the woman said, as she passed the leash to Esmerelda and placed some dog treats in her hand.

"She'll love these."

Toffee snatched toy after toy from the wooden box, bringing each, one by one, to Esmerelda's feet. Then she jumped up into Esmerelda's lap and sat quietly chewing on a fuzzy yellow duck, which seemed to be her favorite toy. Esmerelda felt warm inside as she fed Toffee the dog treats.

"Bingo," the SPCA woman said. "It's a great match, just as I predicted! Congratulations Esmerelda. Toffee is yours!"

Esmerelda kissed Toffee on her head.

At home, Esmerelda tucked Toffee in for the night, carefully setting her in the crate where her mom had put down a soft pillow.
From her bed, Esmerelda watched Toffee cuddle up into a small ball, her eyes closed, and then she was off to sleep in a few minutes.
Esmerelda giggled to herself. I can hear Toffee snoring, she thought, instantly feeling less lonely, but wishing that her dad were there to see her adorable new puppy.

Toffee proved to be the perfect companion for Esmerelda.
Each day they took a long walk to the beach with her mom.
Esmerelda would stop at the water bowl that sat in the midst of all
the RVs parked at the beach. Toffee would noisily slurp, then
energetically run with Esmerelda past the old cement ship, all the way
to the stone wall at the far end of the path. Chasing birds was another
favorite activity for Toffee, paying special attention to the seagulls,
pulling Esmerelda to the sand whenever she spotted one.
On the way home, they would take a short break from walking,
sitting down at a picnic table, where her mom would lay out some
snacks: bits of cheese for Toffee and some peanut butter and crackers for
Esmerelda

Esmerelda started to make friends in her new neighborhood because everyone would stop and want to play with little Toffee.

"Can we pet her?" Children and grownups would ask while Toffee kept her tail wagging the whole time they visited.

Esmerelda started to learn people's names and even met a few kids who would attend her school in September.

One day, about a month after they had adopted Toffee, while on their usual walk to the beach, her mom's cell phone rang just as Toffee started to chase the yellow tennis ball Esmerelda had thrown in the sand. As her mom listened to the person on the other end, Esmerelda could see her face turn very upset. She seemed frightened and started to cry. Placing the phone back in her jacket pocket, her mom sat on a stone bench, her head bent down.

Esmerelda scooped up Toffee and quickly ran over to her mom.
"Mom, what's wrong? Are you crying?" she said.

Her mom wiped tears from her cheeks. "Daddy is hurt, pumpkin.
His leg and head are injured badly. I don't know what will happen.
We need to think good thoughts."
Hearing that, Esmerelda wanted to run and find her father,
but he was so far away. Toffee licked her face as Esmerelda reached
over and hugged her mom.

The walk home was quiet. Esmerelda worried and felt annoyed when she saw people on the beach seem so happy when her dad was in a distant place and hurt badly. She felt scared but comforted by little Toffee, who didn't pull on her leash once going home, seeming to know that something was wrong.

That night, Esmerelda took Toffee from the crate and cuddled her in bed, imagining her dad at home and playing fetch with Toffee.

Would that ever really happen? she wondered. Her mom tiptoed into her room, sat on the bed, and together they prayed for her dad's return, Toffee at their side.

The next day, they heard nothing about her dad and decided to take their usual walk with Toffee. The day was gray, the clouds thick, and a slight drizzle of rain fell from the sky. Holding Esmerelda's hand, her mother said, "You're a big girl now, Esmerelda. You're strong.
We've had to deal with a lot of change lately. I want you to know that I'm proud of how you're handling everything."
Esmerelda squeezed her mom's hand. "Will Dad come home, Mom?" she asked.
"Do you think he'll be okay?"
"I'm not sure, pumpkin, but we need to stay positive," her mom replied.
Toffee tugged on the leash, wanting to play. Her mom threw the yellow tennis ball across the sand. "Come on," she said, "let's show Toffee a good time."

Two of the longest days in her life passed for Esmerelda. She cried
herself to sleep at night. Then, early on the third morning, the doorbell
rang. Toffee barked for the first time, a very loud bark for such
a little dog. Her mom jumped up from the sofa. A gray-haired man
wearing a dark uniform stood at the front door.
Her mom looked nervous.

Behind the man stood Esmerelda's dad, who was leaning on a single wooden crutch, one leg in a knee-high cast, a wide bandage wrapped around his head. Her mom flew past the uniformed man.
Toffee and Esmerelda followed.
"Daddy, I'm so glad you're okay," Esmerelda exclaimed, as she hugged her dad.

Reaching down with one hand, her dad tickled her and said, "That dog was my lucky charm, Ezzie. Your mom sent me photos of you and Toffee. I had to come home as soon as I could to meet her." Esmerelda picked up her squirming puppy and held her up to her dad's face. That's when Toffee licked her dad's nose with her tiny wet tongue.

My granddaughters Kaitlyn and Taylor with Toffee

Acknowledgements

Toffee is the name of my real dog, and I want to thank her for
being the best pet I could ever hope to have.
She came to me via the Santa Cruz SPCA, just like the dog in the story.

Kaitlyn, my gifted granddaughter, helped me to create character traits both
for Toffee and Esmerelda.

Thank you, Kaitlyn.
I love you!

THE REAL-LIFE "TOFFEE"

45428101R00017

Made in the USA
San Bernardino, CA
08 February 2017